ANCIENT CREEK

A Folktale

T0164221

Other books by Gurney Norman

Kinfolks

Divine Right's Trip

ANCIENT CREEK

A Folktale

GURNEY NORMAN

OLD COVE PRESS

LEXINGTON, KENTUCKY 2012

Published by
Old Cove Press
P.O. Box 22886
Lexington, Kentucky 40522

Distributed by
Ohio University Press
30 Park Place, Suite 101
Athens, Ohio 45701
ohioswallow.com

Paperback ISBN: 978-0-9675424-2-3
Electronic ISBN: 978-1-7352242-0-6

for Nyoka

"Think little."

Wendell Berry

Contents

ANCIENT CREEK

A Folktale

ANCIENT CREEK

ONE TIME THERE WAS THIS OLD KING named King George Condominium the Third, sent his army out to conquer a certain mountain district that never had been conquered before.

The old King already ruled about half the world but he wasn't satisfied with just half. He wanted it all. He'd heard that this Hill Domain had a lot of beautiful rivers and valleys and meadows and great herds and flocks of wild game. The mountains had a lot of timber, too, and other natural resources the King was greedy for. So he sent his army down into the hills to dispossess the natives and put them to work as laborers for his empire.

When the King got word that his army had everything in the Hill Domain under control, he decided to go down and look at it, check things over, see what he got. But before he could get started, first one thing then another came up to keep old King Condominium from going.

The King was real busy in those days. His armies were conquering places faster than he could go see them. He had two or three wars going on overseas, and there was a lot of intrigue in the main castle that distracted his mind. The King had two or three mistresses to tend to, not to mention Queen Condominium who was always wanting this and wanting that, she never was satisfied.

So time went along, went along, and old King Condominium got to be an old man, way up in his eighties, and he still never had been to see that part of his kingdom they called the Hill Domain. In fact, the King had just about forgot he even owned a Hill Domain 'til one spring he got sick and his doctor said to him, "Now King, you've got to get away and rest up if you intend to live much longer. You've been working too hard and worrying about things too much, your blood pressure's up, your heart's weak, you've lost your hearing and your eyesight's getting worse every day. The thing for you to do is go off in the mountains somewhere and live quiet for a while. You'll feel a whole lot better if you do."

Well, King Condominium liked that advice. Breathing that pure mountain air and drinking that sweet mountain spring water would surely be a tonic to his system. And no doubt the mountain people with their quaint customs and odd manner of speech and dress would be an entertainment for him and the members of his court.

"Doc," said the King, "go pack your bags. We're all going down to the mountains for a vacation." He told the Queen to get her stuff together and be ready to leave at daybreak. The King ordered his chief assistants to get to work on preparations to move the whole government to Holiday Land, the seat of the Royal Administration in the hills as well as a famous spa.

Then he told his secretary to send word to the Duke of Cumberland, otherwise known as the Black Duke, the Royal Administrator of the Hills, to get ready because the whole royal scene was coming his way fast.

"Oh my God!" the Black Duke shrieked when he learned of the King's impending arrival. "This is a disaster! Hugo! Come in here on the double!"

Hugo limped into the Duke's private chamber on the top floor of the administration building at Holiday Land. Hugo had been wounded in one of the King's wars and his back was drawn over, he walked with a limp and he wore a dark patch over his left eye. The Duke treated Hugo like a dog, but he depended on the one-eyed man utterly. For not only did Hugo possess the physical strength of ten men, he was a brilliant intellect who gave the Black Duke his best ideas and masterminded his most complex and daring schemes.

"Did you get the news?" the Black Duke wailed.

"Yes, Black Duke," said Hugo.

"What are we going to do?" cried the Duke.

"Sire, there is no cause for alarm. Everything is in order to insure that the King and his court will enjoy their time among us, and that upon his departure the King will indeed be well pleased."

"How can you say that?" the Black Duke shouted. "This Domain is a disaster area. The King wants to vacation in these crummy hills, he should've come fifty years ago. The region was a natural wonderland then. The rivers were pure, the timberlands were untouched, wild creatures great and small abounded. Now it's an industrial wasteland. It's the armpit of the empire. The stately trees have been ruthlessly slashed from the hillsides. The mountains have been gutted of their coal and stone and mica and iron and oil and natural gas. The rivers have been poisoned by acid wastes from strip mining. The fish are dead. The game is gone. The air's polluted and the once proud and independent mountaineers have been reduced to vassalage. The King knows nothing of this. He's expecting to find the Garden of Eden, not this insane socioeconomic nightmare."

"Peace, Black Duke," said Hugo calmly.

"Peace?" the Duke snarled. "My own personal head is about to be severed from my body, to be suspended from a flagpole to turn slowly, slowly in the wind, and I'm supposed to listen to you tell me peace?

"Good God, man, don't you know a revolution is brewing in these hills? Don't you know that the rebel outlaw Jack is on the loose again? Haven't you heard the reports from Finley County, where overt acts of defiance against King Condominium's rule have been occurring with alarming frequency? I have been assuring the King for years that all rebellion among the mountain people has been stamped out. If he finds out that I've been lying, falsifying my reports, he'll hang me. Oh, Hugo, what am I to do?"

"Leave everything to me," said Hugo. "I have a plan."

HUGO'S PLAN

"A plan?" asked the Duke.

"A very simple plan, my Lord," said Hugo. "As you know, the King is old and infirm now. His eyesight is failing. His hearing is nearly gone. He will have little strength for venturing to outlying places where he might see the wretched mess that has been made in the Hill Domain. He will want to spend his time in his condominium here at Holiday Land. He will be safe from assassins and troublemakers here. And as the King vacations, so will the members of his retinue.

"They will find diversion enough at Holiday Land's swimming pools, skating rink, tennis courts, squash courts, handball courts, shuffleboard courts, golf course and scuba diving lake, where they may also sail boats, water ski and practice fly rod fishing, after which they will enjoy the sauna, steam room, whirlpool bath, massage parlor, movie theater and billiard room, where guests may also play pinochle, canasta, bridge, poker and other card games, including the curious one played by the local natives called Rook.

"In the mornings they will be enticed by the champagne brunch, and in the evenings made merry by the

9

smorgasbord in Culloden Hall, followed by dancing and drinks in the famous Cumberland Lounge, where the music of Lance Cloud and his orchestra and the comic routines of Skinny Lewis and Bruno the talking dummy are featured nightly."

The Black Duke pursed his lips and thought for a moment. Then he said, "There must be something more."

"Something more, exactly, Sire," said Hugo. "It has already been arranged."

"Arranged?" asked the Duke suspiciously.

"Yes, Sire," said Hugo. "We have arranged a special theatrical performance for the King's amusement, should he show signs of restlessness and have an urge to leave the compound here at Holiday Land."

"Hmm," the Duke muttered as he went to the wall and pressed a small button. A large portrait of King Condominium the Third swung out, revealing a well-stocked liquor cabinet in the wall from which the Duke extracted a bottle of brandy. Pouring himself a drink, he said, "About this plan of yours, Hugo, this theatrical performance, tell me more."

"It's a variety show, Black Duke," said Hugo. "A full evening of comedy and song performed entirely by native mountaineers. It's called *Haw Haw*. I and members of my staff are in control of the script, of course. But the performers will all be hill folk, who are sure to amuse the King with their quaint customs and odd manner of speech and dress."

"Hmm," said the Duke, sipping his brandy. "Go on."

"I guarantee, Sire, that with such entertainment as my staff and I are preparing, the King will have little interest in going sightseeing about the Hill Domain. I can also assure you that when the King has completed his stay with us here at Holiday Land and has returned to his castle rested and fit again, he will not forget that you, the Black Duke, were responsible for his wonderful time in the hills."

The Duke smiled as he poured a brandy for Hugo.

"Hugo," said the Duke, "what would I do without you? Have a drink. Tell me about this *Haw Haw* show."

"Thank you, Sire," said Hugo as he accepted the glass from the Duke. "But better than telling you about *Haw Haw*, why don't you come witness a rehearsal? The natives are rehearsing this very hour."

"Excellent suggestion," said the Duke. As he quaffed his brandy, he said, "I may be wrong about this, Hugo, but I've got a hunch this could be the start of something great."

ThE START OF SOMEThING GREAT

As Hugo and the Duke crossed the central courtyard of Holiday Land toward the theater where the rehearsal was in progress, a dusty messenger ran up, saluted, then handed the Black Duke a sealed envelope.

"What's this?" asked the Duke.

"It's from Captain Heath, Sire," said the messenger. "There's trouble in Finley County."

Turning his back to Hugo and the messenger, the Black Duke broke the seal of the envelope and took out the letter:

> *Sire,*
>
> *Guerrilla bandits have defied the King's edicts in Finley County. Raids have netted several prisoners but many more are still at large. Request reinforcements be sent from Holiday Land immediately to help my outnumbered forces quell these unruly heathen and restore order and respect for the high ideals and values of His Majesty, King George Condominium the Third.*
>
> *Captain Heath, Commanding*

"The vicious devils," the Black Duke muttered. Angrily he crumpled the message into a ball and threw it on the artificial turf at his feet. Then in a firm voice he commanded, "Hugo! Sound assembly! Mobilize the army and all support personnel in the courtyard immediately. We are marching to Finley County to assist Captain Heath in his hour of need. Assemble the entire corps! I want to address all personnel before we march."

The men, women and soldiers of Holiday Land poured from all the buildings and playing fields of the vast complex and dashed to the formation in the central courtyard as Hugo blew the bugle energetically. In a few minutes a thousand red-coated King's Men carrying weapons and full field packs, plus three hundred support personnel, were standing in perfect ranks in front of the Black Duke who was perched on the top step of the armory. The Duke's eyes misted over with pride as he watched the people of his command respond with such eagerness and dedication to whatever cause the Black Duke would announce was theirs.

Around the courtyard were the buildings of Holiday Land, a small outpost of progress in the heart of the alien mountains. The Duke looked at the flag waving grandly from the administration building. He looked at the Grand Arena at the far end of the compound where the great marble statue of King Condominium stood. He looked at the mountains in the distance beyond Holiday Land, at the blue sky beyond the mountains, and at the faint outline of God's visage, barely visible in that nether sphere beyond the sky.

The Black Duke was not a religious man exactly, but he was not utterly devoid of a sense of awe and respect for the Divine Creator who had made the Condominium Empire what it was, and who continued to bless and protect this outpost from the hostile forces arrayed against it.

For as the King himself had once written, there are no atheists among imperialists when the natives are on a rampage.

"Men, women, soldiers and support personnel of the Holiday Land command," the Duke called out in a commanding voice. "I have just received word that the natives are restless in Finley County. Captain Heath has requested our assistance in dealing with some upstart hillbillies who have been so unwise as to defy the edicts of King George Condominium the Third.

"We'll be marching to Finley County this afternoon. So if any of you need to have a quick turn in the whirlpool bath or a double martini on the rocks, you have thirty minutes before we march. We'll be gone an unspecified length of time, so bring extra sunglasses and turtleneck sweaters. Are there any questions?"

"Aye, Sire," an eager social scientist called out from the rear ranks. "Do you think we'll be coming back to Holiday Land before the King arrives? I'm a consultant for the big show we're planning for the King and I have a lot of work to do to prepare for the *Haw Haw* performance."

"Good question," the Duke replied. "Let's see the hands of all people who are in any way involved with preparations for the King's visit to Holiday Land."

Two hundred and sixty-three hands went up, held high by the civilian professional workers in the Royal Department of Development, Tourism and Recreation.

"Excellent," the Duke declared. "You are excused from this expedition. I also want two companies of King's Men to stay behind to guard Holiday Land. As you have no doubt heard, that renegade Jack is on the loose again. He may be so bold as to attack Holiday Land if we let down our guard. The remainder of you will follow me to Finley County. Are there any other questions?"

"Aye, Sire," inquired a psychiatrist who specialized in the Provincial Mind. "Could you tell us what form of transportation we'll be taking to Finley County?"

"We're going to ski," said the Duke.

A silence followed the Duke's remark, broken here and

there by low mutterings and rumblings in the ranks. At last the psychiatrist called out, "But, Sire, it's April. There's no snow on the ground."

"There'd be no snow on the ski slope either if we didn't manufacture it," the Duke replied. "Use your imagination! Since there is no snow on the ground, the rebels will not expect us to arrive on skis. We will simply rig up our snow machine on wheels and have it precede us along the abandoned strip mines all the way from here to Finley County."

"Bravo!" someone in the middle ranks shouted when the Duke announced his idea. Others took up the cry, until everyone in the formation was applauding and cheering the ingenuity of the Black Duke.

The Duke bowed in recognition of the applause. Then he shouted, "Long live King Condominium the Third! All praise to his handiwork!"

And the multitude replied, "Long live the King!"

ONWARD, CONDOMINIUM SOLDIERS

Trudge, trudge, trudge.

Ski, ski, ski.

In spite of the sleet and snow cascading back from the machine, the men and women of the Holiday Land command pressed on, on, forever on, a perfect column of fours winding around the hillsides, skiing behind the huge machine which lay a carpet of white over the barren strip mine spoil banks.

"Onward!" yelled the Duke. "Onward for the King!" The marchers broke into song, a rousing rendition of the anthem that had for generations inspired a nation on the move:

> *Onward, Condominium Soldiers*
>
> *We are marching onwards*
> *Over hill and dale*
> *Which we have paved over*
> *And put up for sale*
> *Natives will not stop us*
> *We will take their homes*
> *While King Condominium*
> *Reigns upon his throne*

18

The Black Duke halted the column and led the marchers in the national cheer:

> *We've put nature on the run*
> *To make the world safe for fun*
> *Yay, rah, FUN!*

The cheer echoed through the narrow mountain valleys as the long column resumed its trek along the pure white carpet of artificial snow.

Captain Heath and a platoon of King's Men met the Black Duke and his legion at the Finley County line. After telling the people of his command to fall out and work on their suntans while awaiting further orders, the Duke and Hugo marched on into the town of Blaine with the Captain, who gave his report as they walked.

"The culprits struck first on Hick's Branch in the Trace Fork area, Sire," said Captain Heath. "Our patrol caught a dozen of them red-handed. Other patrols are pursuing an unknown number who got away. With assistance from your troops we are sure to catch those who remain at large."

"What, exactly, did you catch these culprits doing?" the Black Duke inquired.

"Telling old stories in the forbidden dialect, Sire," said the Captain. "They were sitting around an outdoor fire on a hillside, laughing and talking in illegal accents. Two men were caught whittling strange images from blocks of cedar. Two women were caught with forbidden medicinal herbs drying on racks outside their houses. Another was heard singing a forbidden ballad. One old man was making an unauthorized wooden chair by hand."

"What kind of chair?" inquired the Duke.

"A big rocker, Sire. Made of black walnut, with a bottom of woven hickory bark."

"Treasonous wretch," said the Black Duke angrily. "That's a direct threat to the King's furniture cartel. I trust you dealt with this chairmaker appropriately."

"Aye, Sire, that we did," said Captain Heath with a grin of satisfaction. "Our tribunal has fined him twenty-percent of his protein for five years and sentenced him to lifelong labor in the wood chip factory. The women drying the herbs have been dispatched to Holiday Land to serve cocktails in the Cumberland Lounge."

"And the storytellers?" asked the Duke.

"We dealt with them most severely, Sire. There has been a rash of this kind of subversion. We cut out their tongues and ordered their protein rations reduced by half until further notice. We sentenced half of them to life at hard labor as public relations workers for various imperial enterprises, and the remainder as scriptwriters for an epic film based on the life and work of King George Condominium the Third. Three of the captives have been temporarily spared, Sire, until you have had a chance to interrogate them personally."

"Excellent, Captain Heath," said the Black Duke as Hugo nodded his agreement with these sentiments.

"Excellent work, indeed. I think, however, that sterner measures are called for in the wake of this outrage by the people of Trace Fork. That whole area has become a hotbed of dissent and an example must be made. I want all the people in that hollow resettled in the workers' barracks at Holiday Land, to serve as a labor pool for our coming expansion program. I want all houses, barns, schools, churches, gardens, wells, cemeteries, trees, shrubs, flowers and meadows in that whole valley bulldozed away. Then I want a dam built across the mouth of Trace Fork creek that will flood the entire valley. When the lake has formed, I want townhouses and condominiums built on the hills around to serve as second, third and fourth homes for a thousand King's Men and their families. The surrounding forest region is to be off limits to all native mountaineers forever. Got that?"

"Aye, Sire, it shall be done."

"Good. Now, about these prisoners you're holding. When can I see them?"

"They are waiting for you now," said the Captain. "I'm sure you will find them most interesting."

COLONEL DEED

The Black Duke and his ever present companion Hugo followed Captain Heath into the center of the little town called Blaine. It was just a village really, a single street of stores, shops and business buildings stretched along the riverbank, with a scattering of houses on the hill that rose sharply from the river.

The principal building on Main Street was the old brick courthouse, a relic of the preconquest architecture the Black Duke so despised. The Duke hated dingy little outpost villages like Blaine. He looked forward to the day when the last of them would be razed to the ground and all residences and businesses in the hills would be in centralized compounds such as Holiday Land.

As they approached the courthouse, the Duke turned to go up the steps to the jail, but to his surprise Captain Heath touched his arm and directed him another block on down the street to a grimy office building.

"I thought prisoners were kept in the jail behind the courthouse," said the Duke.

"Ordinarily, they are," said the Captain as they climbed the stairs to the second floor. "But as you will see, we have taken special precautions with these prisoners. I thought it best to say as little as possible about them until we had more privacy, Black Duke. But now that we are alone, I can tell you, Sire, the three young men you will soon interrogate are very special prisoners indeed. We are holding them in conditions of strictest secrecy."

"Explain yourself," the Duke commanded.

Smiling triumphantly, Captain Heath said, "Sire, the prisoners being held just beyond this door are none other than the notorious Will and Tom, brothers of the even more notorious enemy of the realm, the infamous Jack."

"What!" the Black Duke erupted. "You've captured Will and Tom, brothers of the same Jack who for years has remained immune to all efforts of the authorities to capture him and put an end to his rebellious activities?"

"We have, Sire," said the Captain. "The capture of Will and Tom is the most significant development in the history of our efforts to end rebellion in the mountains."

"This is fantastic news," the Duke exulted.

"I knew you would be pleased," said Captain Heath.

"Pleased?" said the Duke. "I'm ecstatic. This is the break I've been waiting for. With Will and Tom in custody, we are sure to lure that rascal Jack into a trap, for it is well known that his loyalty to his brothers knows no bounds. Think of the impression it will make upon the

King if I present him, as a gift, the archenemy of the realm, bound in chains."

"It would indeed be an impressive gesture," said Captain Heath. "Come, Sire. The criminals are waiting."

The three prisoners were being held in the offices of the Broad, Form and Deed Land and Title Company. Broad and Form were away at Holiday Land with their mistresses, but Deed was there—Colonel Deed as he preferred to be called—with two red-coated King's Men who stood above the prostrate forms of the prisoners. The King's Men snapped to attention and saluted when the Duke and his party entered the office. Colonel Deed stood up, but instead of saluting he crossed the room and held out his hand to his old pal the Black Duke.

The Duke and Colonel Deed had been comrades in the great pacification campaigns that had followed the invasion of the hills many years before. He was a lawyer for the Royal Global Energy Corporation now and an officer in the military reserves. Colonel Deed also enjoyed performing occasional police duties in the Hill Domain. When Captain Heath's men captured the three rebels, Colonel Deed had been quick to volunteer his office as a temporary jail and to offer himself as commander of the guard until the Black Duke arrived.

"Well, Colonel Deed," said the Duke as the two men shook hands. "I understand you have some rather special prisoners for me to interview."

"I certainly have," said Colonel Deed as he directed the Duke's attention to the corner of the room where three young men lay in a heap, bound together by chains that held them fast to a radiator against the wall.

The prisoners

One prisoner was unconscious on the floor. The other two were awake but in such weakened condition they could barely lift their heads to see who had come into the room.

"Which ones are Will and Tom?" the Duke asked.

"The ones with their eyes öpen, Sire," said Captain Heath.

"Who is that other wretch?"

"His name is Wilgus Collier," said the Captain. "He lives on Trace Fork among a whole nest of Colliers over there. That's all we know about him so far. He was with Will and Tom when they were apprehended."

"Good work," said the Duke as he walked closer to the prisoners. Holding his nose against the stale odor that arose from their ragged clothes and sweating bodies, the Duke leaned over and shouted in Tom's ear, "Where's Jack?" Then, in Will's ear, he yelled, "Where's your criminal rebel outlaw brother Jack?"

The Black Duke started to kick the prisoners but Hugo moved swiftly to relieve him of that chore. Cuffing the brothers about the head and ears he snarled, "Answer the Duke! Where is your brother hiding?"

The boys opened their eyes and glanced at Hugo, then around the room at the officials who stood regarding them contemptuously. The Black Duke's face was red with anger. Captain Heath looked at them with cool disdain. Colonel Deed grinned at them malevolently. The two King's Men, standing beside the prisoners at parade rest, studied them coldly. Hugo studied them too, but his single eye was not cold. It was alive with curiosity and alertness as it looked first at one brother, then the other. Will and Tom were terrified of Hugo who loomed above them so menacingly. But his face, for all its warts and scars, possessed a mysterious quality that attracted and held the boys' attention.

"We don't know where Jack is," said Will.

"We ain't seen Jack in a long time," said Tom.

"Lying dogs," the Black Duke hissed.

"Treacherous curs," sneered Captain Heath.

"Hated infidels," Colonel Deed snarled.

"Stupid white trash," said the King's Men roughly.

"Unwise peasants," Hugo muttered as he gave each of the young men a fierce shake. Backhanding Tom across the face, Hugo shouted, "Talk!"

"What do you want me to say?" Tom wailed.

"Where is Jack hiding?" the Duke commanded.

"I don't know," Tom answered, holding his hand to his flaming jaw.

"We ain't seen Jack in a long time," said Will.

The Black Duke leaned forward again and almost touched Tom's nose with his own. "Do you mean to deny that you are co-conspirators with Jack in fomenting rebellion against the rule of King Condominium the Third? That you meet with him regularly to plan and carry out your evil design to thwart the King's plans to exploit this mountain region of its last usable tree, its last ounce of coal and oil and stone and mica and iron and natural gas, and its last human being as cheap labor, and then to turn the whole region into a playground for the loyal professionals who have given their lives and talents to the King, so the Condominium Empire can spread not only across the mountains, plains, deserts, lake regions and coastal zones of this continent, but across the entire hemisphere, and finally all the hemispheres of the earth, in preparation for the day when we can then begin to colonize the other planets in our solar system?

"Do you deny that you've been assisting your brother Jack to agitate among the native hill folk, holding illegal assembly, encouraging forbidden language, forbidden arts and crafts, beliefs and activities? Do you deny that you, in league with Jack and other traitors whose names we do not yet know, specifically have a plan to cause disturbances while the King vacations among us next week?"

"We ain't got no such of a plan," said Tom.

"Then, who organized the treasonous, hedonistic, pagan, ritual orgy on Trace Fork night before last? Was that not part of your revolutionary program?"

"Why, that was just folks getting together," said Tom.

"Just neighbors associating," said Will.

"Banding and confederating, you mean," Colonel Deed said contemptuously.

"Did you have forbidden discussions about the old days?" Captain Heath interjected. "Did you use words in the forbidden dialect that may have evoked unauthorized images in the mind of an earlier, more pagan time?"

"We talked about kinfolks some," said Tom.

"We talked about the old homeplace some, if that's what you mean," said Will.

Hugo kicked Will with the side of his foot. "Do not make stupid jests in the presence of the Black Duke!"

But even as he snarled, even as he kicked, something in Hugo's face, something behind his eye, communicated a subtle message to Will. Something in his manner made Will suddenly unafraid, even as Hugo kicked him and Tom several times more.

"This is getting us nowhere," the Duke said. "Shoot them full of truth serum. Give them sodium pentothal. I'll teach these oafs to withhold information from a representative of the King."

Hugo expressed serious reservations about administering a potion as strong as sodium pentothal to prisoners in such weakened condition.

"Bah!" said the Duke. "What do I care about the condition of these foolish peasants? Fill their veins full. Let's hear what the wretches have to say."

The assistants to Captain Heath administered the sodium pentothal to Wilgus. Soon after, the Black Duke began the interrogation.

"What is your name, young man?" asked the Duke.

"I am my father's son," Wilgus replied.

The Duke slapped Wilgus across the face with his leather gloves. "Idiot! That's no answer. Tell me your name. What were you doing in the company of two notorious rebels on Trace Fork the night of the pagan ritual orgy around the campfire?"

"Miracles, signs and wonders," came the reply.

"Impertinent fool!" shouted the Duke, striking Wilgus again with his gloves. "Answer the question!"

Hugo touched the Duke lightly on the arm. "Perhaps the prisoner is speaking in subtleties," said Hugo. "If we

31

listen, we may find secret codes in the strange things that he says."

"I have no time for subtleties," the Black Duke snarled. "I want the story. Talk, you peon! Sing!"

And Wilgus began to sing:

I love to tell the story
Of unseen things above

"What insanity is this?" the Duke protested. But Hugo held up his hand. "Listen!"

And Wilgus began to speak in a dreamy monotone:

I'm in a mine, huddled at the face with no light, it's
total dark around. I can breathe all right but the air
is sulfuric, stale, I have to adjust, grow gills in my
neck, become a kind of fish in order to live this deep
underground.

"What gibberish!" shouted the Black Duke, suddenly losing all patience. He turned from Wilgus toward Tom, who was deep in a trance by now, ready for questioning.

"Let's hope this one makes more sense than that other idiot," said the Duke, somewhat calmer now as he took his seat again by the couch where Tom lay. "Are you Tom, brother of the legendary rebel outlaw Jack?" asked the Duke.

"Yes."

"Do you confess to being one of the mountain people

seeking independence from the rule of King Condominium the Third?"

"Yes."

"What is the name of your rebel band?"

"We ain't got no name that I know of," said Tom.

"Of course you've got a name!" the Duke shouted. "All rebel bands have names. What are you anyway, the Freedom Fighters of the Hills? The Hillbilly Liberation Front?"

"We're just folks that live around here," said Tom.

"Do you admit that you seek to overthrow the dominance of the Condominium Kingdom?"

"Oh, we'd like to do that all right."

"Who has taught you such treasonous attitudes?" the Duke demanded.

"Didn't nobody have to teach us," said Tom. "It come to us from our ancestors."

"Liar!" the Black Duke shouted hysterically. "Don't you realize that you've been given sodium pentothal and sodium pentothal makes you want to tell the truth? Tell the truth! Where is your outlaw brother Jack hiding?"

"Aye, he's probably over yonder on Ancient Creek."

"What?" the Duke shouted. "What's this? Where?" The Duke turned and motioned for the guards and assistants to gather close around. "Where did you say?"

"Ancient Creek," said Tom. "He's probably over there staying with Aunt Haze."

"Where is this Ancient Creek?" the Duke demanded. "I never heard of it."

"It's way back in the hills," said Tom.

The Black Duke searched the faces of his assistants. All of them shook their heads and shrugged.

"We've never heard of Ancient Creek," said the Duke. "I've never even seen it on a map."

"Ancient Creek don't show up on maps," said Tom. "It's too far back in the hills."

"Well, who is this Aunt Haze person you mention? Is that some kind of code name?"

"Oh, no," said Tom. "That's her real name."

"Is she your aunt?"

"Well, she ain't my personal aunt," said Tom. "She's kind of like everybody's aunt. She's real old now, Aunt Haze is."

"How old?"

"Well, they don't nobody know for sure," said Tom. "Some say she's over three hundred years old."

The Black Duke slapped Tom with his open hand this time. Then he grabbed him by the shoulders and shook him hard. "You're trying to make a fool of me!" the Duke shrieked. He was so enraged he gasped for breath.

Hugo handed him a glass of water. When he had sipped it and rested a moment, he went on.

"This Ancient Creek," said the Duke. "What makes the place so special? Why would Jack hide there?"

"Oh, it's a beautiful place," said Tom. "The creek runs down off this high mountain, through these big woods, then down along a big green meadow where the animals come to feed. There's lots of flowers and birds and critters running around. They come right up and talk to Aunt Haze. Aunt Haze talks to the creatures all the time."

Without warning the Black Duke pounced on Tom and began to pummel him with his fists. "Lying dog! Insufferable pig! Insult the Black Duke with fairy tales, will you? Offend the intelligence of the Royal Adminis-trator of the Hills with outrageous nonsense, will you? You'll die for this treason! I'm going to kill you myself!"

And the Duke would have, too, if Hugo and the guards had not pulled him away from the helpless Tom.

To ease the Duke's frustrations, Hugo proposed an alternate plan for the capture of Jack. "Sire, why not let one of the prisoners go free so he may carry word to Jack of the terrible plight of his brothers? Jack is sure to attempt a rescue. If we are unable to go after Jack, let's arrange for the fool to come to us."

A wave of relief spread across the Black Duke's face

as he listened to Hugo's proposal. The Duke agreed to Hugo's plan instantly. Will was selected to be set free. He had not yet been doped up with truth serum.

The guards removed the chains from Will's body and escorted him out of the building to the main street of Blaine. As soon as they released him he took off running for the woods at the edge of town. Later that evening the Black Duke and his entourage returned to Holiday Land, dragging Wilgus and Tom along in chains.

GOOD NEWS

Except for the nagging matter of Jack, all was in readiness for the King's arrival at Holiday Land. The Royal Suite had been redecorated to the last detail. New purple carpets covered the floor from wall to wall. New orange drapes hung over the sliding glass doors that opened onto the balcony overlooking the central courtyard of Holiday Land. New chartreuse wallpaper of an avant garde design adorned the walls. New Formica furniture had been installed, including a king-size bed with a Magic Fingers vibrating unit that operated free of charge.

Flags, banners, colorful decorations of all kinds gave the streets of Holiday Land a festive air. All the King's horses and all the King's men wore sparkling red uniforms, and the men and women among the administrative personnel sported the latest fashionable attire. The local people who did the routine work around Holiday Land had been issued new work clothes and given a ten percent increase in their protein that made their faces gleam with ruddy health. Sumptuous feasts had been prepared, enormous stores of wine had been laid in. Holiday Land had never looked so lovely as it did now on the eve of King Condominium's arrival.

Had it not been for the gnawing threat of Jack and his rebel companions, the Black Duke would have been overcome with joy and satisfaction. But as it was, there was a corner of his mind that was a nervous wreck. The Duke cursed Jack for denying him the kind of confidence and serenity he felt he deserved in this, his entire life's crucial hour. He cursed the stupid prisoners for the uselessness of their statements. The Duke lay in bed planning cruel revenges on his prisoners when suddenly the door flew open and Hugo rushed in, breathless with excitement.

"Sire! Sire! Good news! Good news!" Hugo shouted through an enormous smile that revealed his stained and broken teeth.

"What's the meaning of this intrusion?" the Black Duke snapped.

"Pardon, Sire," said Hugo, bowing deeply. "But I am certain the news I bring will be a tonic to your nervous disorders. I am pleased to report, Sire, that the capture of Jack is imminent, and the end of the revolution is a foregone conclusion no later than this time tomorrow night."

"How can this be?" the Black Duke asked, throwing aside his satin sheets to don his velvet robe. "What has happened to bring about such a favorable turn of events?"

"It is most fortuitous, Sire," said Hugo. "While you were sleeping we recaptured Jack's brother Will that we set free five days ago. He was attempting to enter Holiday Land disguised as a kudzu vine. Knowing that time was of the essence, we promptly took him to the interrogation room and administered truth serum to him.

"Under our questioning he revealed that his brother Jack planned to attempt a rescue of his brothers on the night of the King's arrival. In addition to liberating all political prisoners, the fiend intends to embarrass you, the Black Duke, in the eyes of the King, thus undermining your position as Royal Administrator of the Hills."

"Impetuous fool!" the Black Duke sneered. "What preposterous impertinence."

"The poor peasant plays into the palms of our hands," said Hugo gleefully.

"Precisely," said the Duke proudly. "When I catch him, I shall have no pity on the plebeian wretch. I shall punish him and all the pathetic people who persist in perpetuating his pernicious rebel program. I shall repay him for all the pain he has caused me. Let him plead for pardon. Let him pray his pagan prayers. I shall not be prevented from putting him through tortures so pure..."

"Ahhh, wait," said Hugo. "The Duke has yet to hear the best portion of our plan."

"Please proceed," said the Black Duke. "I'm certainly well pleased with all you have presented so far."

"I propose, Sire, that we use the full potential of our opportunity to turn the tables on Jack," said Hugo. "I propose that we manipulate Jack's own plans and have him hoist himself by his own petard. I propose, Sire, that we arrange for you to personally apprehend Jack right on the stage during the big show tomorrow evening, before the very eyes not only of King Condominium and all his retinue, but in full view of the people of Holiday Land who will be in attendance.

"We'll write parts in the play for Will and Tom, and that creepy Wilgus as well, then place them onstage as a lure. Jack will be unable to resist this opportunity to liberate his brothers and humiliate you in the process, but we'll be waiting for the peon, fully prepared to pounce like powerful panthers."

The Black Duke danced a little jig of joy. "Hugo, you're a genius."

"All I know I have learned from you," said Hugo humbly.

"You have learned well," said the Duke. "And when this is all over I shall see that you are richly rewarded."

"Thank you, Sire. In the meantime, there is much work to be done to complete the details of our scheme. It would be well if you could witness a rehearsal of the *Haw Haw* show so that we can find a place to write Will and

Tom and Wilgus into the script. The natives are due to begin a rehearsal within the hour. Perhaps you would like to attend."

"I shall be delighted," said the Duke. "I'm having lunch with Captain Heath and Colonel Deed today. I'll bring them with me."

"Very good, Sire," said Hugo. Hugo bowed, then hastened across the compound to the Grand Arena.

haw haw

Hugo used the hour before the dress rehearsal for a final touch-up of *Haw Haw*'s opening skit, in which a mountain man named Abner Little has a tobacco-spitting contest with a man named Snuff Jones.

The official script called for the contest to be a draw until each tries to perform the traditional feat of spitting tobacco juice while simultaneously drinking moonshine from a jug. Abner performs this feat with ease, but Snuff chokes and drops the jug to the ground. Snuff emerges triumphant, however, when the falling jug dents the earth and strikes oil, making him an instant millionaire, which enables him to leave his farm to go live happily ever after in Holiday Land.

As Hugo critiqued his performers after the run-through of the first skit, the Duke, Captain Heath and Colonel Deed, merry from the wine and scintillating conversation of their lunch, entered the theater and took seats in the front row, where the King would sit during the performance. The Black Duke was vastly amused by the rehearsal.

"Haw, haw, haw!" the Duke roared. And Colonel Deed and Captain Heath echoed his laughter.

"As soon as the first act of the skit is over," Hugo explained, "Will and Tom and Wilgus will be dragged onto the stage and dumped in a pile, front and center. That will be the signal for Jack's assault."

"Is that Jack ever in for a surprise!" said Captain Heath.

"I can hardly wait," said Colonel Deed.

"I will have a platoon of King's Men ready to meet them," said the Duke as he passed around his brandy flask for an early toast to their coming victory.

The King's Arrival

Hurrah! Hurrah!
Welcome King Condominium the Third!
Welcome Lovely Queen!
Long Live the King and His Mighty Host!
Royal Court! Dukes! Nobles!
Princes! Princesses!
Elegant Gentlemen and Ladies!
Pleasures and Delights Await You!
These Decorations, Fireworks, Music
And Great Throng of People
Welcome You to Holiday Land!

King Condominium was exhilarated by the tumultuous welcome given him by the people of the Hill Domain. His old ears could not hear their cheers, but he could see them, lined twenty deep along the roads and streets of Holiday Land.

How happy they seemed!

How shining were their faces! How adoring were their eyes as they gazed upon his royal personage.

And what a lovely place it was. The fiberglass houses, so clean, the artificial turf lawns, so litter free, the plastic trees that lined the asphalt boulevards, so tidy and dust free. Oh, how wise of the doctor to send me to this remote outpost of the kingdom, thought the old King. Oh, what a tonic it is for my tired body and low spirits! How very excellent of the Black Duke to prepare such a reception for my arrival.

And how clever it is of the Duke to arrange a theatrical performance in my honor this very evening. How splendidly thoughtful it is of him to spare me the ordeal of yet another dreary state banquet and the fatiguing chore of making small talk with a bunch of sycophants and nincompoops. How brilliant of the Duke to divert us all with a stage show, a program of native wit and music. An evening of delightful surprises. Black Duke knows my taste well. A man as bright as he could rise high in my empire. Yes, he could. A man as sharp as he could become the next director of the Almighty Regional Commission. He might even become director of the True Values Authority someday.

After the King and Queen had rested in the Royal Suite, the servants and ladies-in-waiting entered to help the Royal Couple into their evening clothes. Then, as the sun was going down behind the mountains, the King and Queen set out together for the Grand Arena, followed by fourteen dozen members of the court.

ChE BIG Show

As the King and Queen entered the theater, ten thousand people stood and began to sing "Condominium
Kingdom, My Condominium Kingdom" at the tops of
their voices. King's Men and officials of the Royal Bu-
reaucracy of the Hills filled the forward seats of the giant
hall. Their impression was one of elegance and confidence
and pride as they watched their monarch walk majesti-
cally down the center aisle.

The other half of the audience was made up of local
people. Dressed in their daily work clothes, they were
less brilliant in appearance than their masters but they
formed a solid mass in the rear seats that was pleasing
for the King to behold. He could not hear well enough
to tell that the applause from the back rows was less
enthusiastic than that from the front. But he could see
their arms waving and their hands moving.

"Splendid," the King said as he walked down the aisle
toward his seat. "It's going to be a wonderful show."

ShERMAN WAGNER

The men who were to portray Abner Little and Snuff Jones were in full hillbilly costume when they came onstage. They wore overalls and straw hats and Snuff carried a moonshine jug. But once they had taken their places front and center on the stage, Snuff set the jug on the floor. Then instead of turning toward each other and going into their comic routine, the men looked out at the audience.

The man who was to play Abner said, "Good evening, everybody. My name's Sherman Wagner. You probably know that none of us in the show tonight are professional actors or anything. We're just folks that live around here. The Duke and Hugo thought it would be a good idea to have us onstage to entertain the King and his court when they came to visit Holiday Land. Everybody in the show has worked hard to get their parts ready. We hope everybody in the audience has as good a time this evening as all of us intends to."

The Black Duke, who was seated in the front row beside the King, glanced uneasily at Hugo, who sat in the aisle seat beside the Duke.

Hugo smiled at the Duke. "They're just ad-libbing a little to amuse the King," he whispered reassuringly.

The happy expression on the King's face seemed to confirm Hugo's statement. The Duke was pleased to see the King sitting up straight with a big grin on his face as he studied the ragged mountaineers on the stage.

"What I thought I'd do," Sherman said, "is introduce the other people in the cast tonight. And I'll start with my old buddy here, Landon Frazier. Landon, why don't you say a few words to the people?"

RAMONA CAMPBELL

"My name's Ramona Campbell," the woman said. "I'm fifty-three years old. I've lived in these hills all my life, through good times and bad. But I have to say there's been a lot more bad times than good.

"Last fall, they's a bunch of guys from the Royal Global Energy Corporation come on my mommy's land at the head of Rainy Creek, started bulldozing her pasture away to get at the coal underneath. I asked 'em what they were doing. They said the government had declared the coal-fields a national sacrifice area, that the minerals under the ground were more important than the people that lived on top of it.

"I started to say something else but before I could get a word out, five big laws come up, grabbed me by the arms, drug me off to jail, beat me black and blue. The leader was ol' J.P. Bunyan, biggest coward in the history of the mountains. He's probably out there in the audience right now, hearing me call him that. I hope you are, J.P., I want you and everybody else in this big auditorium to know that I called you a coward that's got rich off the land and coal and labor of the poor people of these hills."

The applause for Ramona's speech was general throughout the back seats of the arena, and this time several King's Men stood up to scowl at the people behind them. Unable to hear as he was, King Condominium couldn't make out what was going on exactly but he could feel the excitement in the room and it thrilled him. He understood now. This was all part of the big show! What a fantastic show! The King hadn't been entertained this well in years.

"Jolly good show, old chap!" said the King to the Duke. "Jolly good show!"

The Black Duke thanked the King. But his attention was on the people onstage who were deviating from the script so outrageously.

"This treasonous farce must not continue!" the Duke said to Hugo. "Put a stop to it at once."

Hugo nodded. "I'll sneak around backstage and see what I can do."

"Get those prisoners out there on the stage," commanded the Duke. "It's time to spring our trap on Jack!"

"Aye, Sire," said Hugo as he slid out of his seat and limped off through the door that led backstage.

ᴄʜᴇ ᴛʀᴀᴩ

Soon after Hugo went backstage, Will and Tom and Wilgus came out and took their places next to the others who had spoken. A buzz of excited conversation rose above the audience when the three young men appeared. The native people looked at each other and grinned while the King's Men in the front rows looked at each other in bewilderment and consternation.

As Will stepped forward to speak, the Black Duke saw Captain Heath leading a platoon of Red Coats toward the stage. Ah ha, thought the Duke. At last the trap is sprung!

A hush fell as Will cleared his throat to speak. "Good evening, everybody. My name's Will. I'm Jack's brother. This here is my other brother Tom, and this is Wilgus Collier, a friend of ours from over Trace Fork way. We've had a pretty hard time this week. The Black Duke's had us in jail the past few days and he's been pretty heavy on us. So we ain't up to making any long speeches. Let me just say that in my opinion this whole Holiday Land outfit is a crooked scheme that has taken the lands and homes away from the people who live here and built an evil enterprise on it. Everything about this stupid Holiday

Land is fotched on. I think we ought to do like Mother Jones said, which is to pray for the dead and fight like hell for the living!

As soon as Mother Jones' words were out, everyone in the back rows of the arena leaped to their feet cheering and shouting and whistling and applauding furiously.

The Black Duke and all his minions jumped to their feet and started babbling to each other excitedly. By now Captain Heath's platoon had reached the stage. When the King saw the soldiers going up the steps he cackled in glee and poked the Duke in the ribs with his elbow.

"Black Duke, this is the finest show I've ever seen," said King Condominium. "You've thought of everything. You've left out nothing. You're a genius, my boy, and I'm going to reward you for it. How'd you like to be director of ARC?"

Before the Duke could answer, a second squad of Red Coats ran past them down the aisle. "It's just fantastic," the old King shouted to the Duke above the rising pandemonium in the arena. "Black Duke, you can even be director of TVA if you want to."

"I want to," the Black Duke replied. But the Duke's words were drowned in the noise that was rising all around. King's Men were on the stage now, attempting to put handcuffs on Ramona Campbell who resisted furiously until a Red Coat smashed her in the shoulder with his rifle butt. Other soldiers lashed out at Will and Tom and Wilgus, at Stella and Sherman and Landon, at all the mountain people within range. Landon sank to the floor with a bleeding head. Tom grappled with two King's Men to protect Sherman who had thrown himself across Wilgus to shield him from further blows, while Stella clawed the face of a soldier who was swinging at Tom. The fight was fairly even until the second squad of soldiers reached the stage from the right. They swarmed over the battered natives, swinging their guns like clubs. But then from the wings came a charge of other mountain people to join the fray, a good dozen of them who pounced on the startled soldiers and flailed away.

The fight itself was astounding enough for the Black Duke. But what was utterly incredible to him was the fact that among the charging natives was Hugo, fighting the soldiers with his fists. There's got to be some mistake, the Duke thought as he saw his faithful assistant Hugo pull two soldiers off the prostrate forms of Wilgus and Landon and hurl them into the orchestra pit.

This behavior is definitely not part of the script, the Black Duke said to himself. Then he yelled, "Hugo! Hugo! What in God's name are you doing?"

Hugo paused in his combat for a moment to look down

at the Duke from the stage. Swiftly he stripped off his eye patch and stood up straight. Then with both hands he removed the hideous mask that had covered his face and threw it aside.

Through a grin of triumph, the young man thus revealed said, "My name's not Hugo, you fool. I'M JACK!"

"Kill him!" the Black Duke screamed, and a soldier's voice yelled, "Fire!"

Gunshots.

Curtain.

Dark.

People screaming, rushing for the doors, soldiers, natives, men and women of the court pushing, all bolting for the exits, squirting out in streams through doors and windows.

"Fire!"

Ragged volleys, muzzle-flashes winking in the dark.

Jack falls to the stage floor, shot through the arm and side.

Ramona falls beside him, moaning.

Sherman falls, two bullets in his leg.

A bullet creases Stella's neck as she yells, "Fight for the living!"

Struck on the head by a rifle butt, explosions ring in Wilgus' mind like blasting in a mine.

I'm in a mine, huddled at the face with no light. I can breathe all right but the air is sulfuric, stale, I have to adjust, grow a kind of gills in my neck, become a fish in order to live this deep underground. It's so dark I believe I don't have eyes until a prick of light comes toward me through the pitch black dark of the mine. It's like foxfire. It's like a spark from two thoughts striking one another. It's like the first star that ever was.

Slowly the light floats toward me, bearing a promise to drill my forehead like a breast auger, like a mine drill. Shavings coil out like old memories, form shapes around the light. They form my father with a carbide lamp on his head. They form my mother wearing a shiny brooch at her throat and then they become Jesus carrying a candle that becomes a minnow and swims away through the mine's dark river. I can't see it but I hear the river gurgling. I panic trying to decide whether to follow or stay where I am.

Follow, says a voice within the water. Come with me.

I huddle against the face of the coal, wondering if my eyes are open or closed.

They're open, says the voice within the water. Come with me.

Face down in dark water, I see ancient ferns, tall as tipples a million years ago beneath the sea. As the water lightens I see a firmament arise, a lovely wilderness of plains and valleys and mountains, with creeks flowing

*in the valleys past woods and meadows, past bottom
land where willows grow, and sycamores, and muskrats
in their holes and turtles in the mud and kingfishers
swooping low across the water as the sun goes down,
filling the sky with orange and purple light.*

*The water is amber-colored now. I see minnows in it,
I see a perch swim by. I see brilliant pebbles on the bottom,
and green waving grass beneath the water. I see a sandbar
reaching out from the shore. My feet sink into it. Planted
there, I rise from the water like a tree, a flowering shrub
with gnarled branches, thick with leaves, adorned by
blossoms white as clouds, moist with the dew of a brand
new April evening.*

*Before me is a clearing, surrounded by trees, a green
meadow marked in the center by an ancient stone, gray
and weathered, writing on it obscure as hieroglyphics.*

*See the stone, says the voice within the water. And
beyond the stone, see that old woman coming out of the
trees, see the wounded people limping along behind her
in bunches of twos and threes, helping each other along
the way.*

See Stella.

See Ramona.

See Sherman Wagner.

See Will and Tom, carrying their brother Jack.

And see yourself among them, Wilgus, among the wounded, following old Aunt Haze as she walks across the meadow past the stone, walks on toward the dogwood tree that stands by the waters of Ancient Creek.

Now hear Aunt Haze as she leads the people to the tree. Gather around, she says. Gather beneath the dogwood. Sit in a circle, rest yourselves. I'll go to the woods and get some herbs to doctor your all's wounds.

ANCIENT CREEK

The brown mole watched Aunt Haze cross Ancient Creek on stepping stones and enter the woods on the other side. Haze looked the same as she had forever, an old woman with a walking stick, black shawl around her shoulders, long white hair flowing down. But there was something unusual about Aunt Haze this afternoon. It was the way she walked. She was walking fast, in a hurry, headed somewhere quick. When she came by the brown mole's burrow, the mole stood up and said, "Aunt Haze, how come you're running through the woods in such a hurry?"

"Hello, Mole," Aunt Haze replied. "I was hoping I'd run into you. I've got some wounded people over by the dogwood tree. I'm looking for a lin root to use in some healing salve I'm making. Do you know of any lin trees nearby?"

"Sure," said the mole. "I was digging under one just the other day. Come on and I'll take you to it."

The mole led Aunt Haze on into the woods until they came to a lin tree.

"Thank you, Mole," the old woman said. "This is the very tree I need."

And Aunt Haze bent over and started to dig in the ground with the end of her walking stick.

"Here, Aunt Haze, let me do that," said Mole. Before Haze could reply, he commenced scratching and rooting in the loamy forest floor. In a few minutes he exposed a long sturdy root about a foot deep in the ground.

"That's wonderful," said Aunt Haze. "Now if we just had something to cut that root with."

"Let me bite it through for you," said a beaver who had strolled in from the creek to see what was going on. "I can bite through a lin root in a jiffy."

With a few quick bites of his large buck teeth, Beaver cut the root and handed a length of it up to Aunt Haze.

"How come you want this lin root, Aunt Haze?" asked Beaver.

"Well, I'm going to make a salve and heal some wounded people," said Aunt Haze.

"Who are the people?" asked an owl perched in the top of a nearby oak tree, listening to all that was said.

"They're friends of mine from over in the settlements," said Aunt Haze. "There's been trouble over there. I'm trying to help them out. In fact, Owl, I wonder if you'd do something for me?"

"What do you want me to do, Aunt Haze?"

"I need you to fly across the mountains to the settlements and spy out what's going on over there," said Aunt Haze. "These wounded people's in need of news. Could you go over and see what you can find out for us?"

"I'll be glad to," said Owl. And with a flap of his wings he flew away to begin his errands.

Aunt Haze thanked the lin tree for the gift of the root. She thanked Mole and Beaver for their help. Then she set out through the woods toward the meadow again, where the wounded people were waiting under the dogwood tree.

the ceremony

Wilgus watched Aunt Haze prepare the healing salve. He watched her scrape the bark and skin from the lin root into a bowl, then chop it fine with her knife. Aunt Haze added some comfrey leaves and sassafras bark and some jellico root she carried in her pouch.

"What we need now is some water from Ancient Creek," Aunt Haze said. She handed Tom a cup and told him to go to the creek and fill it. When he came back with the water, the old woman poured a few drops into the bowl, then set the cup aside. As she stirred the potion she chanted, *sha lahn tah, sha lahn tah, roon lah lune.*

After a while Aunt Haze said, "Okay everybody, scoot in close now and I'll doctor your wounds."

With her fingers Aunt Haze smeared the healing salve on Wilgus' forehead. She put salve on the bullet wound in Stella's neck. She treated Ramona Campbell's wounded shoulder and Sherman Wagner's leg, and several bruises that Will and Tom had on their bodies.

Aunt Haze set the bowl aside and picked up the cup of water. She handed the cup to Will and told him to take a drink and pass it around for the others to drink from, too.

When the cup returned to Aunt Haze she sipped

from it. Then she said, "Now let's help ol' Jack get him a drink. Lift his head up there, Wilgus. Rest it on your knee. I'll hold the cup to his mouth."

Gently, Wilgus raised Jack's head and slid his leg underneath it. Jack's eyes were closed and his lips were pale, and his breathing was so shallow his chest hardly moved. But Jack's flesh was warm. There was life yet in him. When Jack sipped the water, his eyelids fluttered open briefly and he looked into Wilgus' eyes.

Jack tried to sit up then but Aunt Haze said, "Lay still. We're not finished yet."

Gently, she applied the salve to Jack's arm and the terrible wound in his side. Then she directed Wilgus to lay Jack on the ground again and move back to his place in the circle. Wilgus watched Aunt Haze stretch out her arms and hold her hands over Jack. Three times she circled her hands above his head, chanting *sha lahn tah, sha lahn tah, roon lah lune.*

Aunt Haze sat awhile with her eyes closed. Then she motioned for all the people in the circle to move in close to Jack and place their hands on him. When everybody was in place, close to Jack, Aunt Haze held Jack's face in both her hands and said, "Shhh, now. You all listen."

The rushing sound of Ancient Creek nearby grew louder in the night. The water made a music, there were voices in it. There was moonlight on the water, breaking on the rushing waves and tiny sprays that flashed around the rocks and caught the rays of the full moon in the sky. From somewhere far away in the darkness, an owl began to hoot. The sound of the owl and the rushing sound of the water rose and fell against each other for a long time. Then they both faded as Aunt Haze spoke again.

"This meadow here by Ancient Creek is my family's old burying place," Aunt Haze said. Her voice was low and strong as a storyteller's now, warming to the tale. "It's a wonder-working power place on the ground that people have been coming to for more generations than I know about. There's just the one gravestone out yonder in the meadow to mark it, but all my people are buried here. My ancestors from way back in the ages are all laid here. And I'll be buried here myself one day.

"It's a powerful place. Power flows right out of the ground on Ancient Creek. It flows from the water sounds and the air around. It flows down on us from the dogwood tree above. It passes through our bodies as we sit here, through our hands, out into Jack. It's helping to heal poor Jack. Time the sun comes up tomorrow, Jack's going to be good as new. All of us are. For as we let the power flow through us to him, it runs around our circle and gives us new life, too.

"We all need new life and strength for there's a sight of work to do. You all heard the owl hoot a while ago. That was my friend Owl telling what he found out over in the settlements today. He says people all over the hills are in resistance to the King now, and that a big struggle has started.

"He says Landon Frazier has taken his old farm back and that he means to keep it this time. He says Landon's already started planting nut trees on the ski slope, and he plans to get a crop of sorghum in his bottomland. The King's Men are ganging up to stop him from doing that and so the word's gone out all over the hills for the people to come and help Landon reclaim his farm.

"So you'll be getting up early tomorrow and going back over the mountains, back to the settlements to help Landon. By sunrise you'll all feel good again, ready to hike the hills and go back and stand with him. The thing for us to do right now is lay down close to Jack and keep him warm."

Wilgus and Stella and Sherman and Will and Tom and the others all lay down and snuggled in close to each other on the ground. When they were settled, Aunt Haze took off her shawl and spread it over the people. Then she went around the circle, tucking it in.

Most of the people went to sleep as soon as they lay

down, but Wilgus stayed awake awhile. Snug among his fellows, he lay beneath the mantle, looking up at the moist moonlight on the blossoms of the dogwood tree.

The white tree flowers were what he saw.

What he heard was the water rushing by.

He heard voices in it.

> *I love to tell the story, sang the water,*
> *Of unseen things above*
> *Go to sleep now, said the water,*
> *Go to sleep and dream lah lune*
> *Dream sha lahn tah*
> *Dream lah lune*

Living into the Land

Jim Wayne Miller

GURNEY NORMAN'S *Ancient Creek* is a conspicuously successful instance of a work of fiction that is regional in its setting, character, and orientation, and yet is Aesopian in the universality of its import. Norman's *Ancient Creek* demonstrates how it is possible for a contemporary writer to be immersed in the traditional culture of a region and yet not be limited, oppressed, or weighed down by that immersion.

Norman is traditional in the true sense of the word. "Traditional" is popularly misunderstood to mean something akin to "static" or "unchanging." But the word derives out of the Latin *traditio*, a handing over or down. In writing *Ancient Creek*, Norman begins with a resource handed down from his place and people, the Jack Tale. But Norman's Jack Tale *Ancient Creek* is different from any other Jack Tale that preceded it. He takes what he needs of the Jack Tale tradition, what of it he finds useful for his purposes, and goes on from there, inventing. His traditionalism is not static, but dynamic. Any genuine traditionalism allows for innovation. The word "traditional" as it is popularly misunderstood means something closer to "antiquarian."

Norman's use of a folk narrative form indigenous to his region does not prevent him from bringing to bear all that he is capable of knowing and thinking and feeling. And his range is wide. Within the conventions of the Jack Tale, Norman spoofs and parodies regional and national history, including government agencies and their consultants and "change agents"; academia and the "helping professions," represented by the psychiatrist who is a specialist in the Provincial Mind; popular culture and its stereotypical representations of the region and its people; the American middle class, its assumptions and love of gadgetry and paraphernalia; and the international dimensions of the capitalist economic system. His style is as flexible as his subject matter is varied, ranging from the simple profundity of fable, as we know in Aesop, to the stinging allusive satire reminiscent of George Orwell's *Animal Farm*.

Just as he is traditional in the true sense of the word, Norman is also original, understood not as presenting us with something new, a novelty, but in the sense of returning to origins and original purposes. In *Ancient Creek* Norman functions as writers originally functioned. The first writers, those composers of epics and sagas, the great stories of the Bible and other holy books, were people who recounted significant events from the tribal history. They reminded their audiences, through poems and stories, of the exploits and achievements of the ancestors, presented both positive and negative models, dramatized the dilemmas and conflicts encountered in life, and highlighted the values members of the community considered worth living by and dying for. These writers examined life with imagination.

This original role of the writer has been obscured in the modern era, though that role remains essentially what it has always been. In *Ancient Creek*, Gurney Norman reminds us that the writer exists in a community and in a certain relationship to that community and, just as centuries ago, the writer examines human life with imagination, asking his or her audience to consider who we are and how we got to be the way we are, who our ancestors were, what they believed and why, what is valuable in and about life, what life means, ultimately.

Given this relationship to audience, the writer knows that he or she is not altogether free to invent, in arbitrary fashion, poems, stories and dramas. The stories the writer tells, the conflicts, dilemmas, values and attitudes examined are in large part givens, present already in the collective experience of the community. The writer knows also that he or she does not stand apart from the story to be told, but is a part of the story, which may not be the strikingly novel invention of the writer but rather an older story that has been evolving for a long time, a story not entirely unfamiliar but whose meaning we need to be reminded of.

Norman's *Ancient Creek* is timely and timeless. The story is rooted in a particular place and set of circumstances and draws on a particular storytelling tradition; yet its import has global applicability—all of which is a way of saying that it is regional in its materials, method and manner, but universal in meaning.

While the concepts of region and regionalism are

undergoing reexamination and reevaluation, and while there is less of a tendency to view regions and regional traditions as aberrant, the critical reception of regional writing leaves much to be desired. The word regional, when applied to imaginative writing, remains for the most part a term of relegation. But the altered intellectual climate permits the possibility of literary history and criticism that deal more discriminatingly with regional writing. Critics are freer to distinguish between what Eudora Welty has called "the localized raw materials of life" and "their outcome as art."

In time it may be widely understood that our regions are not surviving remnants of the past but part of our present—and of our future. Our regions may become more distinct as time passes and may come to be seen, as Donald Davidson saw them, "as a process of differentiation within geographic limits . . . predestined in the settlement of our continental area." Our regions are not passing away so much as they are emerging. For the genuine expression of a place and its people, as Mary Austin knew when she wrote in the 1930's, ". . . comes on slowly. Time is the essence of the undertaking, time to live into the land and absorb it; still more time to cure the reading public of its preference for something less than the proverbial bird's-eye view of the American scene . . ."

The past is not a fad. The past, as Faulkner pointed out, is not even past. It is still happening in the formation of our regions. In the future, where we are will continue to have something to do with who we are, just as who we are will depend in part upon who we were. We cannot set aside an awareness of the past as if it were the fashion of one season. As José Ortega y Gasset reminds us: "To excel the past we must not allow ourselves to lose contact with it; on the contrary, we must feel it under our feet because we have raised ourselves upon it."

To see the regional as universal requires not only intimate knowledge of a place or locale, but knowledge that extends through time, resulting in a historical perspective. We are still in the process of living ourselves into the land and absorbing it; we are still learning to feel the past under our feet. As a continuous form of government, the United States is an old country, but we are still young as a land and people. In the conclusion of *Walden*, Thoreau asserts: "We know not where we are." Most people, he says, "have not delved six feet beneath the surface [of their place], nor leaped as many above it." The agenda suggested in Thoreau's conclusion, and echoed in Frost's "The Gift Outright," remains an appropriate agenda for us.

In Gurney Norman's *Ancient Creek* we have a model for getting on with this agenda. His narrative is the result of his having lived into his region and absorbed it, of having felt the past under his feet. His ability to present the regional as universal in this story is attributable, in part, to his intimate knowledge of his place and people, and to his appreciation of the past as something more than a fad.

Perhaps there is still time for literary critics and historians to help readers learn to prefer rooted diversity to rootless uniformity. Perhaps the time will come when we will have torn down the fence between the regional and the universal, and the old error will no longer need correcting; when book reviewers will routinely distinguish between books of a region and books merely about a region. When that time comes, it will be easier for readers and reviewers alike to see the regional as potentially universal.

'I'M JACK!'

KEVIN I. EYSTER

*It is only the story ... that saves our progeny from
blundering like blind beggars ... The story is our escort;
without it, we are blind. Does the blind man own his
escort? No, neither do we the story; rather, it is the
story that owns us.*

Chinua Achebe, *Anthills of the Savannah* (1988)

THE HISTORICAL substance of *Ancient Creek* is cultural survival, and one means of survival is what Norman
calls "the Jack quality," a quality he contends contributes
to "a living society." This quality is something more than
Jack's "cleverness." Norman sees it "as a psychic energy...a
resilience, a problem-solving but also inspired quality" in
which "we are not resigned to tragic fate." His literary

transformation of the Jack quality from oral tradition, it can be argued, is grounded in the pre-Socratic, Sophistic notion of *doxa*.[1]

According to Bernard Miller, "*Doxa* can be understood as the practical wisdom inherited from tradition, that collection of beliefs, convictions, and attitudes we accept for no other reason than that they are anchored in some more or less coherent way in our cultural system." Miller's argument rests on the assertion that the Platonic definition of *doxa* as being mere "opinion" is reductive and shortsighted. Via Martin Heidegger's interpretation of the term, Miller explores how *doxa* "parallels" both "Christian theology" and "arete, the classical ideal of excellence."[2] To gain a sense of Norman's use of *doxa* in relation to the Jack quality, the writer's personal and artistic connections to Appalachia become important.

Norman maintains that "deep in the most remote mountains [of Appalachia] is a kingdom that is integrated" and harmonious. Such a mountain kingdom is envisioned in the concluding scene of *Ancient Creek*. Norman believes this story reconciled him with his "hillbilly background," a process that includes "participating in a revival of interest in the oral traditions of my native Appalachian region."[3] He describes his growing interest in Appalachia in detail:

From about 1973 to 1978 it was not unusual for me to go from my weekly session with my female Jungian analyst in California on Tuesday, a session in which I would explore memories and feelings left from my growing-up years in Eastern Kentucky, and then on Wednesday board a plane and fly to Kentucky and set forth on a weeklong round of visits of family and friends that would carry me on a route linking Berea, Hazard, Whitesburg; Wise and Lee Counties, Virginia; and Boone, North Carolina, including nearby Banner Elk and Beech Mountain where I knew resided the master tale-tellers of the region, if not the continent... [B]y the time I would catch my plane back to California on Monday, I would feel nourished in some deep, soul way, as if I had drunk from a fountain that truly never did run dry. In part the sense of nourishment came from connecting so deeply with the mountain landscape, with friends, with the music and the tales which we claim as our own. But in addition, I was certain, and still am, that the renewal of feeling came from the very power of the tales which we had immersed ourselves in for several days.[4]

At the heart of his story, "deep in the most remote mountains" of Appalachia is the "fountain that truly never did run dry" and the mythic figure Aunt Haze. Aunt

Haze's use of the healing lin root and water from the "ancient creek" represents what political theorist Herbert Reid sees as the central theme of Norman's work: "the healing power of the landscape."[5] Norman consciously incorporates his Appalachian cultural heritage in *Ancient Creek*. Through his use of the Jack tale tradition, he draws upon the "beliefs, convictions, and attitudes"[6] of this heritage.

II

C. Paige Gutierrez concludes from her study of Marshall Ward's Jack-telling that virtually all Beech Mountain Jack tales are episodic; that they unfold incrementally; and that, drawing from Vladimir Propp's morphology, they are "unified by a 'lack/lack liquidated' structure."[7] Gutierrez indicates what Jack achieves:

Jack's actions in the episodes [of a tale's body] are directly related to the elimination of the lack [the introduction] of the frame story. The liquidation of the lack usually demands that Jack leave home and return home. The lack is always liquidated; that is, Jack is always successful. The liquidation of the lack demands that Jack use trickery or receive magical aid. The use of trickery or magic distinguishes a clever tale from a magic tale.[8]

Jack's success lies in his ability to integrate elements of cleverness or magic through his actions, all of which are brought to life by the tale tellers like Ward and writers like Norman who continue to sustain the storytelling tradition.

As a literary work, Norman's story is not structured like actual Jack tales. [9] Readers might conclude that the story's series of scenes are episodes, but none are repeated or developed incrementally. It does conclude optimistically, however; and, although what Jack and his comrades lack (the dispossession of their land) is not fully liquidated, their experience at Ancient Creek, according to Norman, enables them to become "renewed and revived." While Norman's narrator opens the story formulaically by framing the conflict that follows, he does not begin with an image of the young Jack but rather he begins with the image of the old king, King Condominium the Third.

Written in 1974 as the Vietnam War was coming to a close and the Nixon regime was ending, the story can be read as political allegory, a critique of the oppressor and champion of the oppressed. The setting is not Asia or Washington DC but Appalachia, and the acts of oppression become, symbolically, strip mining and absentee ownership. The conflict that unfolds is between the dispossessed Appalachians and the outside forces who turn this once majestic mountain kingdom into "Holiday Land," controlled by Condominium's chief assistant, the Black Duke. What brings the confrontation to a head is the anticipated arrival of the ancient Condominium, who has never visited the hill domain before. Since Jack is initially referred to by the Black Duke as "the rebel outlaw Jack" who is "on the loose again," his real identity is not revealed until two-thirds of the way through the story. In *Ancient Creek*, Jack is no longer a child or a naïve young farm boy; he is older now, and the fight for this existence is the fight for a region as well as a way of life.

As a trickster figure, Jack is disguised as Hugo, servant of the Black Duke, who must appease both the King and the Black Duke while setting a trap for them. He suggests they keep Condominium in Holiday Land and away from the despoiled hillsides by having the local natives present a special theatrical performance called *Haw Haw* in which the natives parody themselves. While the oppressed natives are practicing their performances, Hugo accompanies the Black Duke and his soldiers to the village of Blaine, where three culprits, Jack's brothers Tom and Will and their friend, Wilgus Collier, are being held by one Captain Heath. The natives have been caught engaging in such "forbidden" acts as "singing a forbidden ballad...[and] making an unauthorized wooden chair by hand." Those dealt with most severely are the storytellers, who face having their tongues cut out and then either serving as public relations people or writing a script for "an epic film based on the life and work of King Condominium the Third."

The prisoners—Tom, Will, and Wilgus—are interrogated and kept alive in hopes of discovering where the rebel Jack is hiding. Tom tells them that his brother is probably hiding "over yonder on Ancient Creek." The imperialists have never heard of Ancient Creek. Tom describes it as a place "too far back in the hills" to show up on maps. Ancient Creek, a remote area of Appalachia untouched by the advancement of secular progress, is set in sharp contradistinction to Holiday Land.

Hugo uses the performance of *Haw Haw* as a means of direct revolt. While Condominium, virtually deaf, is caught up in the show, the Black Duke realizes something is amiss because the natives are not acting out the script. While speaking in their own voices, they articulate serious complaints against Condominium's regime. A bloody battle ensues, in the midst of which Hugo reveals his true identity. But the battle takes its toll; Jack the trickster is wounded, shot through the arm and side.

In the final three sections of the story, Norman aligns his narrator with a particular character so that the final scene in *Ancient Creek* is filtered through the eyes of

Wilgus. The protagonist in Norman's collection of short stories, *Kinfolks,* Wilgus is given the culminating vision in *Ancient Creek.* Having been knocked unconscious by the Royal soldiers, Wilgus Collier, true to his name, enters the personal unconscious and, by extension, the "collective unconscious." He envisions the rebels making their way to Ancient Creek and the magical world of Aunt Haze. Wilgus' journey into the subconscious psyche reveals the means by which the natives seek to solve the predicament they must return to and face in the conscious world.

Although the body of the narrative never returns to the frame story as actual Jack tales do, the clever, now wounded Jack, through the perspective of his compatriot Wilgus, enters into a magical "other world," and Norman places this other world in the heart of Appalachia.[10]

To survive, to be able to attempt overcoming what they lack, these nonconformist mountaineers turn to the traditional values embodied by Ancient Creek and imbued by Aunt Haze. In Proppian terms, Aunt Haze is the "donor" of a "magical agent," a procedure that takes place under a dogwood tree. Wilgus' vision is an ancient ceremony in which Aunt Haze heals the wounded with the lifeblood of the actual creek. As the practitioner of folk medicine and folk religion, the earth mother, the goddess of nature, Aunt Haze is the very embodiment of folk wisdom and *doxa*. For Aunt Haze as well as Jack, Wilgus and the rest, their cultural survival, to appropriate Miller's apt phrasing, "turns on how [they] stand ... relative to the light of *doxa* as exemplar[s] of the virtues that constitute the social fabric [of Appalachia]."[11]

Significantly, belief in the Jack quality extends beyond Jack to the community and the land, and is given voice through Aunt Haze. To the Jack qualities of cleverness and good fortune, perseverance and resilience, Aunt Haze adds belief in kinship and the importance of place. In the face of continuous exploitation, "the manner in which these beliefs are vitalized in action ... must be continually sustained and proved through struggles and suffering."[12] Such qualities enable Jack and his allies to gain sustenance and strength under the legendary dogwood tree. Aunt Haze's passing of "the mantle" to them suggests future promise and potential for cultural renewal, including renewal of the land itself.

III

For Norman, *Ancient Creek* is not only a staging of the dehumanization of Appalachia, which the work clearly portrays; it is a means of uniting a region, of disseminating a regional self-awareness, but an awareness with universal and cosmic ramifications. As a literary artist, he uses his understanding of the Jack tale tradition to advance the story line in *Ancient Creek,* to endow his mountain characters with Jack qualities, to provide thematic structure to the story, and to defend Appalachia while raising serious questions about the nature of mainstream America.[13] At the same time, Norman decisively pays homage to his heritage through yet another form of American *doxa* in which he persuades his readers to participate in the power of story once again:

I have had a marvelous gift bestowed upon me by my culture; this part of America that we are talking about now, the Southern mountains, the Appalachian region. I have been the beneficiary of its power, as part of a living process of cultural transmission that goes on to this day, and this includes the writers as well as the folk artists. At every stage of the development of this funny old tale I've had many collaborators. Many people have participated, you see...I see us all, scholars included, as part of the audience of the tale. All of us, if we are lucky, will gather around Aunt Haze's dogwood tree.

NOTES

* Unless otherwise noted, all quotes by Gurney Norman from a personal interview with the author, April 4, 1990, Lexington, Kentucky.
1 The concept *doxa* takes on different meanings for different rhetoricians. Roland Barthes, for example, explores the concept negatively throughout his autobiography as a "triumphant discourse": The *Doxa* (a word which will often recur) is Public Opinion, the mind of the majority petit bourgeois Consensus, the Voice of Nature, the Violence of Prejudice. *Roland Barthes by Roland Barthes*, trans. Richard Howard (New York: Farrar, Strauss and Giroux, 1977). We can call (using Leibnitz's word) a doxology any way of speaking adapted to appearance, to opinion, or to practice. Miller's more affirmative definition of *doxa*, it seems to me, connects positively to Norman's subversive use of it against "petit bourgeois Consensus." Both Barthes' platonic and Miller's sophistic definitions reinforce the centrality of language as we use it to create our imaginative worlds. Bernard A. Miller, "Retrieving a Sophistic Sense of *Doxa*," *Rhetoric in the Vortex of Cultural Studies*, ed. Arthur Walzer, proceedings 1992 Fifth Biennial Conference, Rhetoric Society of America (Minneapolis: Burgess, 1993), 32-41.
2 Miller, "Retrieving a Sophistic Sense of *Doxa*," 32-35.
3 Gurney Norman, "A New Look at Old Tales," *Appalachian Heritage* 33 (1986), 25.
4 Ibid., 25.
5 Herbert G. Reid, class lecture, University of Kentucky, April 30, 1990.
6 Miller, "Retrieving a Sophistic Sense of *Doxa*," 32.
7 C. Paige Gutierrez, "The Jack Tale: A Definition of a Folk Tale Sub-Genre," *North Carolina Folklore Journal* 26 (1978), 86. In "The Literary Unity of Ray Hicks's Jack Tales," W.H. Ward's analysis reinforces Gutierrez's study. Ward reiterates an important generic distinction: "One of the crucial...points to be made about [Hicks'] versions of these stories is that they show a strong inclination to

present Jack's triumphs as the result of his canniness or his good fortune, not a mixture of the two." W. H. Ward, "The Literary Unity of Ray Hicks's Jack Tales," *North Carolina Folklore Journal* 26 (1978), 130. William Lightfoot's entry on "Jacks Tales" in the *Encyclopedia of Southern Culture* lists certain "Jack qualities": . . . skill, courage, industry, perseverance, imagination, independence, and a propensity for attracting good luck and supra-normal assistance. The consistency and frequency of the association of these traits with Jack essentially define the subgenre. William Lightfoot, "Jack Tales," *Encyclopedia of Southern Culture*, eds. Charles Reagan Wilson and William Ferris (Chapel Hill: University of North Carolina, 1989), 506-07. The world of Jack and Aunt Haze suggests two key folktale motifs: F111, "Journey to earthly paradise:; and F715, "Extraordinary river." Stith Thompson, *The Folktale* (1946; reprint, Berkeley: University of California, 1977), 429-93. As the recasting of the traditional Jack tale into a nontraditional form, *Ancient Creek* is significantly a written narrative with both clever and magical elements. For a discussion of present-day tellers of Jack tales as well as collections of their tales, see William McCarthy, *Jack in Two Worlds: Contemporary North American Taletellers* (Chapel Hill: University of North Carolina, 1993).

8 Gutierrez, "The Jack Tale," 106.

9 See, for example, *Outwitting the Devil: Jack Tales From Wise County, Virginia*, ed. Charles L. Perdue, Jr. (Santa Fe: Ancient City, 1987). which includes twenty-eight Jack tale texts.

10 For discussion of the magical "other world," see Vladimir Propp, *Morphology of the Folktale* (Austin: University of Texas, 1968), 53; Max Luthi, *Once Upon a Time: On the Nature of Fairy Tales* (Bloomington: Indiana University Press, 1976), 70, 115; and Linda Degh, "Folk Narrative," *Folktale and Folklife*, ed. Richard Dorson (Chicago: University of Chicago, 1972), 63.

11 Miller, "Retrieving a Sophistic Sense of *Doxa*," 36.

12 Ibid., 36.

KEVIN I. EYSTER

13 Norman's story depicts a reconciliation of forces alive in Appalachian culture, Jack and his compatriots must overcome an evil king and his bourgeois society desirous of destroying all things native. Such a society represents a machine-like existence, a secular society without belief in anything sacred. I am reminded of Robert Pirsig's discussion of "Quality" in *Zen and the Art of Motorcycle Maintenance*, specifically the passage addressing mankind's predisposition to separate from and lord control over nature: *And now he [Phaedrus] began to see for the first time the unbelievable magnitude of what man, when he gained power to understand and rule the world in terms of dialectic truths, had lost. He had built empires of scientific capability to manipulate the phenomena of nature into enormous manifestations of his own dreams of power and wealth—but for this he had exchanged an empire of understanding of equal magnitude; and understanding of what it is to be part of the world, and not an enemy of it.* Robert M. Pirsig, *Zen and the Art of Motorcycle Maintenance* (New York: Bantam, 1981), 342. Clearly, the event occurring at the close of *Ancient Creek* depicts a scene in which the participants have become "a part of the world, and not an enemy of it."

WORKS CITED

Achebe, Chinua. *Anthills of the Savannah*. New York: Bantam, 1988.
Barthes, Roland. *Roland Barthes by Roland Barthes*, trans. Richard Howard, New York: Farrar, Strauss and Giroux, 1977.
Degh, Linda, "Folk Narrative," in *Folklore and Folklife*, ed. Richard Dorson, 60-73. Chicago: University of Chicago, 1972.
Gutierrez, C. Paige. "The Jack Tale: A Definition of a Folk Tale Sub Genre," *North Carolina Folklore Journal* 26 (1978): 84-109.
Hicks, Ray. "Jack and the Three Steers," *North Carolina Folklore Journal* 26 (1978): 75-79.
Lightfoot, William. "Jack Tales," *Encyclopedia of Southern Culture*, eds. Charles Reagan Wilson and William Ferris, 506-07. Chapel Hill: University of North Carolina, 1989.

Luthi, Max. *Once Upon a Time: On the Nature of Fairy Tales*. Bloomington: Indiana, 1976.

McCarthy, William B. *Jack in Two Worlds: Contemporary North American Taletellers*. Chapel Hill: University of North Carolina, 1993.

Miller, Bernard A. "Retrieving a Sophistic Sense of *Doxa*," *Rhetoric in the Vortex of Cultural Studies*. ed. Arthur Walzer, 32-41. Proceedings, Fifth Biennial Conference. Rhetoric Society of America. Minneapolis: Burgess, 1993.

Norman, Gurney. "Ancient Creek," *Hemlocks and Balsams* 9 (1989): 9-51.

— "A New Look at Old Tales." *Appalachian Heritage* 33 (1986): 24-27

— Personal Interview. April 4, 1990.

Perdue, Charles L. Jr., ed. *Outwitting the Devil: Jack Tales From Wise County Virginia*. Santa Fe: Ancient City, 1987.

Pirsig, Robert M. *Zen and the Art of Motorcycle Maintenance*. 1974; Reprint New York: Bantam, 1981.

Propp, Vladimir. *Morphology of the Folktale*. Austin: University of Texas, 1968.

Reid, Herbert. Class Lecture. University of Kentucky. April 30, 1990.

Thompson, Stith. *The Folktale*. 1943, reprint Berkeley: University of California, 1977.

Ward. W. H. "The Literary Unity of Ray Hicks's Jack Tales," *North Carolina Folktale Journal* 26 (1978): 127-33.

REAÐING 'ANCIENC CREEK'

ANNALUCIA ACCARÐO

"FEEL FREE to make any changes," wrote Gurney Norman, the author of *Ancient Creek*, to encourage me in
translating the folktale into Italian:

> *Rewrite passages and translate freely: now you are
> the narrator. It is in the nature of the work that the
> text is neither sacred nor frozen, but living—as in
> the oral tradition—where every narrator adapts the
> story to their own style, to the situation in which
> they live and to the people who are listening to it.*

The spirit of this folktale, which has its roots in the Appalachian tradition, is entrusted to the multiple transformations of folklore's process of creation and collective recreation, so that the narration returns to the point of departure enriched by the new contexts through which it has traveled.

In *Ancient Creek* the traditional material of folklore (Jack the rebel is Jack the Giant-Slayer, protagonist of Kentucky's most popular series of folktales) is used to transpose the history of the "colonization" of Appalachia into fable form. All the necessary ingredients are there: on the one hand, the old king, obtuse and greedy, with his even more obtuse administrators; on the other, the weak, who manage to stand up to their oppressors through recourse to cunning and solidarity. They are strong because of their cultural tradition, which has its roots in nature. It is a story of defeats, revolutions and renewal. The historical references are precise. On the one hand there is Appalachia; on the other, American capitalism, which applies a policy of colonization at home while enacting a policy of imperialism abroad.

Yet other deeper elements can better explain the additional meanings offered by the story. The mandala design on the cover of the first recording of *Ancient Creek*— which features images of a white dogwood blossom, a gravestone, the moon and the earth—suggests a process of reconciliation, a dynamic image of synthesis, represented by a circle contained within a square.

The privileged form in this process of reconciliation is the telling of stories. As the shaman cures the ills of the mind by telling the stories of creation myths, so the storyteller, Norman says, opens by means of his stories, the paths to memory, throwing light on hidden aspects of human experience.

The function of the word is particularly important in a culture such as Appalachia which has its roots in a great oral tradition, of which storytelling is a central expression. Storytelling is a spontaneous process of communication, a universal art form common to all without distinction of instruction or environment. It is the instrument by which one expresses oneself and communicates in a narrative form. By giving form to experience through its narration, not only can new meaning emerge, but it can be interpreted and transmitted so that the experience lives on. In this way the individual comes into possession of the community's experiences, its traditions and memories. Particularly in Appalachian culture, telling stories has signified and signifies keeping history alive, feeling part of a community, and constructing a collective memory.

The first transcription of *Ancient Creek* appeared in

the journal *Hemlocks and Balsams,* with articles that debated the relationship between regional and universal literature and explored the question of whether a contemporary writer can participate extensively within the culture of his region without being trapped by it. Drawing its roots from a storytelling tradition and speaking of the problems of a particular place, *Ancient Creek* nevertheless manages to convey meaning that transcends the local problem. For example, the description of Appalachia as a region polluted and damaged by strip-mining—and abandoned by young people in their search for work— echoes Eliotian images to the extent that it assumes an apocalyptic tone.

In the process, Norman plays on the ironic combination of elements of modernity and narrative forms from oral folk tradition. The performance which Hugo stages in honor of King Condominium is entitled *Haw Haw,* a laugh which refers back to a television program with the title *Hee Haw,* an imitation of the donkey's bray to which the mountain people are likened. As in the TV series, so the intention of Hugo's performance is to amuse the king by presenting the mountain people "with their quaint customs and odd manner of speech and dress." This phrase adds hilarity and suggests corrosive irony against stereotypes.

The link between folktale elements and current political relations is no less strong, between folktale and social context. But just like in the mandala, the clear connections between the folktale and social reality do not exhaust its meaning. When the process of reconciliation involves the personal level, then it tends also to re-establish a psychological equilibrium which had disappeared; it tends to heal a fragmented ego. As the mythic characters of folklore and literature fall to the bottom of the well or are swallowed up by the whale, so Wilgus, after being knocked on the head, imagines going through a mine to reach Ancient Creek, that legendary place: Appalachia before modernization. The descent into the mine becomes a metaphor for the descent into one's own self, a journey to the center of the earth by which the protagonist can rediscover himself through the various strata of social experience, towards its very roots, right down to the contact with nature and back up again. For this reason it is important that the traditional mine signals the moment of realization, as opposed to strip-mining which instead provokes the destruction of the land. So contact with nature is fundamental in this process of reconciliation:

E gli apparve una distesa di pianure e montagne,
con torrenti che scorrevano nelle valli fiancheggiate

*dai boschi, da pascoli e da salici e aceri. L'acqua
ha il colore dell'ambra, è piena di pesci, ciottoli
brillanti sul fondo e alghe verdi sotto l'acqua. Poi
si trovò davanti un cespuglio coi rami pieni di
foglie e di germogli inumiditi dalla rugiada di una
sera di aprile. Di fronte, una radura circondata da
alberi. Un prato verde, con al centro una pietra,
grigia e istoriata di oscuri geroglifici.*

*As the water lightens I see a firmament arise, a
lovely wilderness of plains and valleys and mountains, with creeks flowing in the valleys past woods
and meadows, past bottom land where willows
grow, and sycamores, and muskrats in their holes
and turtles in the mud and kingfishers swooping
low across the water as the sun goes down, filling
the sky with orange and purple light. The water
is amber-colored now. I see minnows in it, I see a
perch swim by. I see brilliant pebbles on the bottom, and green waving grass beneath the water. I
see a sandbar reaching out from the shore. My feet
sink into it. Planted there, I rise from the water
like a tree, a flowering shrub with gnarled branches, thick with leaves, adorned by blossoms white
as clouds, moist with the dew of a brand new April*

evening. Before me is a clearing, surrounded by
trees, a green meadow marked in the center by an
ancient stone, gray and weathered, writing on it
obscure as hieroglyphics.

Nature, tradition and history (represented by the stone inscribed with hieroglyphics) together contribute to a healing of wounds and a restoration of strength.

In the magic kingdom of Ancient Creek, there lives old Aunt Haze, a person tied both to the land and to tradition, who hands out the magic potion, helped by the animals. They are all seated in a circle; Aunt Haze invites the wounded to drink the water of the stream and to rest by drawing strength from the land where their people are buried.

La zia Haze aveva l'aspetto che aveva sempre
avuto

Haze looked the same as she had forever. . .

. . . questa terra è piena di meraviglie di forme e
di forza. La gente torna qui a guarire da tante
generazioni che nemmeno io posso ricordare. C'è
soltanto una tomba al centro del prato, ma tutta
la mia gente è vissuta qui e sepolta qui, genera-
zioni e generazioni indietro nel tempo, e anch'io

un giorno sarò sepolta qui. È un luogo pieno di forza e di suggestione. La vita sgorga dal terreno lungo Ancient Creek, scorre verso di noi attraverso la sanguinella, passa nei nostri corpi e nelle nostri mani mentre stiamo qui seduti. E domani, quando sorgerà il sole, saremo rigenerati. Abbiamo bisogno di nuova vita e di nuova forza. C'è ancora molto da fare.

It's a wonder-working power place on the ground that people have been coming to for more generations than I know about. There's just the one gravestone out yonder in the meadow to mark it, but all my people are buried here. My ancestors from way back in the ages are all laid here. And I'll be buried here myself one day. It's a powerful place. Power flows right out of the ground on Ancient Creek. It flows from the water sounds and the air around. It flows down on us from the dogwood tree above. It passes through our bodies as we sit here, through our hands, out into Jack. It's helping to heal poor Jack. Time the sun comes up tomorrow, Jack's going to be good as new. All of us are. For as we let the power flow through us to him, it runs around our circle and gives us new

*life too. We all need new life, and strength, for
there's a sight of work to do.*

At this point the rite of healing can be considered complete
through contact with oneself, the land, nature and not
least, the word, tradition and history.

In the case of this rite, whoever reads, listens or sees
Ancient Creek has passed without interruption from
folktale and oral history (the local people as "witnesses"
in the performance organized for the benefit of the King)
to autobiography (Wilgus Collier is a character who ap-
pears in other autobiographical stories by Norman). From
contemporary narratives that draw on the reappropriation
of folk culture, the story suggests, a movement can spring
to reclaim resources and construct egalitarian relation-
ships between people.

OCTOBER 30, 1975

DEE DAVIS

IN 1975, when Gurney came to the loft to read *Ancient Creek* for June Appal Records, Appalshop had not been split as much as it had been strategically divided. The original storefront on one side of town housed (to the extent you could say that) the administration (to the degree you could say that), the film office, the darkroom, the magazine, and the required degree of disapprobation to keep the operation in line.

On the other end of Whitesburg's main drag, built into an upstairs corner of a former Dr. Pepper plant, were the offices of the record label, the theater company, and four thousand square feet of open planking replete with enough cable-spool chairs and tables to outfit an all hours hangout for traditional musicians and hillbilly hipsters.

I remember it as a transitional time. The Appalshop Board had voted unanimously that all decisions need no longer be unanimous. The guys at the loft were given their own business checkbooks so they would stop spending everyone else's money on beer. And it was during this time that I had been eased out of my job at the magazine because of my incompetence.

Gurney's place within the Appalshop framework was special. He had grown up in Perry County, Letcher County, and Lee County in Virginia. And somehow he had figured out how to live the artistic life in the San Francisco Bay area without ever losing his accent. He was a feeler, a name conferred on the devout. When his novel *Divine Right's Trip* was at its peak (published in *The Last Whole Earth Catalog* and, by extension, displayed on every milk-crate coffee table in America), Gurney handed the movie rights to Appalshop and its unlikely troupe of twenty-something media entrepreneurs. Some agent must still cringe. And when the big screen version never materialized, he shrugged it off with no discernible sign of losing faith or patience.

Gurney coming to town to make the record was considered a big deal. His arrival was anticipated as if he were a literary character himself, somewhere between Godot and Hickey the Iceman. During the year, Appalshoppers sent him cards, letters, and on one snowy day a twenty-foot scroll written on butcher paper. In the missives were jokes and tales and an occasional call for help. He was a counselor to those of us having a tough time, an enabler to those birthing big ideas, and an exemplary role model for the competent and incompetent alike.

The night that Gurney read *Ancient Creek* was an Appalachian artistic be-in. I sat with my pal Marty among the spools and drank Falstaff beer as people began to make their way into town and up the shaky stairs. It is funny what you remember, but Falstaff was considered the worst beer, and I knew if I bought it I had a decent shot at hanging on to my purchase until the guys with the checkbooks drained everything else on the premises. I remember a young girl overhearing my conversation with Marty and asking if the two of us had been to college. She said we sure sounded like we had. Ah, to be young and too eloquent by half.

There were a lot of people there I didn't know. Marty pointed out Ed McClanahan when he arrived. I knew of Ed from his articles in *Playboy*. He showed up wearing western boots and a cowboy hat, a far weirder sight in that crowd than the tie dye and overalls we were used to. The others that came are a bit of a blur (and some of them I later married). But by the time we started, the place filled up with writers, actors, filmmakers, photographers, full-time activists, and musicians of various stripes—a live audience reclining on every square yard of a not-al-together-sanitary, mostly yellow shag carpet.

We were advised not to open beers while Gurney was reading. There would be bathroom breaks, so we were told to sit tight, hold it in. We could cheer if the mood hit.

Then we were shushed. And I remember Gurney's reed-like voice rising up and taking us away, off to where Jack, Will, Tom, kings and giant developers, writers in cowboy hats, young girls and loquacious beer drinkers, could share the shag carpet and a momentary enterprise unlike any we would likely see again.

The Story of
Ancient Creek

Gurney Norman

THE STORY of *Ancient Creek* began in July of 1974 while I was living in a small cottage on a bluff overlooking the Pacific Ocean in Mendocino County, California. The ocean mirrored the sky, a vast single blue expanse. There were no other houses around. There was no automobile traffic that I could see or hear. The cottage had no television or telephone and I read no newspapers. The only sounds were the wind blowing in off the ocean and the cries of the seagulls. The pure beauty of the place may have helped me imagine pristine Ancient Creek itself, "so far back in the mountains it doesn't show up on maps," a natural wonderland, unmarked by human beings.

Certainly the Mendocino County coast was a comforting place to be in the summer of 1974 as the final weeks of the Watergate story wore on in the nation's capital, leading to President Nixon's resignation August 9. My one communication device that summer was a radio. The Watergate story and the narration of President Nixon's departure came to me in the oral tradition, into my ear, not my eye. My imagination pictured the final scenes of the fall of the imperious King.

I had gone on retreat to Mendocino County to try to finish a book of short stories that I had contracted with Random House to publish in 1975. It had not occurred to me to write a satirical folk myth until I was a dozen pages into it. I should have written Kurt Vonnegut a thank you letter for his contribution to the story of *Ancient Creek*. In my second week in my cottage, I read *Slaughterhouse-Five* and *Breakfast of Champions* and they affected me mightily. During the closing episodes of the Watergate story, satire, irony, absurdity and freedom from the burden of strict realism were available to me as never before. Sometimes the political realm of social affairs is so absurd that fantasy is required to deal with it.

I had brought other books with me to my coastal cottage, mostly having to do with mythology and folktales. Since my school days I had kept handy my copy of *South from Hell-fer-Sartin,* Kentucky folklorist Leonard Roberts' collection of Kentucky mountain folktales. I also had my well-marked copy of Joseph Campbell's *The Hero with a Thousand Faces,* as well as *The Interpretation of Fairy Tales* by Marie-Louise von Franz. I had brought *Grimm's Fairy Tales* and Paulo Freire's *Pedagogy of the Oppressed.*

For purposes of writing and reading and thinking and dreaming, my situation in Mendocino County was as good as it gets.

Early in 1975, I called my friend Jack Wright, a founding member of June Appal Recordings, a division of Appalshop in Whitesburg, Kentucky. Appalshop was and continues to be a nonprofit multidisciplinary arts and education center that produces original films, videos, theater, music and spoken-word recordings, as well as educational experiences for young people in the Appalachian mountains. I called Jack to propose that June Appal publish *Ancient Creek* as a spoken-word album. Even though my *Ancient Creek* story was a tightly written piece, I thought that presenting it as a story one hears instead of reads would place it in some proximity to an oral tradition. I had grown up in the Cumberland Mountains not far from Whitesburg and even though I had lived in California for a number of years, I had always thought of the Appalachian region as home. I was well aware of the music and story traditions of the mountains, particularly the many tales about the clever boy hero named Jack. Jack Wright has some of the clever qualities of the mythical Jack himself and he readily agreed that we should record *Ancient Creek*. We set October 30 as the date to record the story.

Dee Davis' finely written reminiscent essay, "October 30, 1975," captures the essence and spirit of the recording session that memorable night, when fifty or sixty people gathered in June Appal's studio to have some fun as we recorded *Ancient Creek*. This was a special group of people. Many of them knew a great deal more about writing and storytelling and music and the performing arts than I did. We had a unifying thing in common, which was that most of us had grown up in the surrounding mountains and had come from more or less similar backgrounds. For me, it was a deep experience of feeling at home after years of living away. I still had many living relatives in the mountains. My grandmother, mother and an uncle lived just over the mountain in Lee County, Virginia. I felt that everyone at the recording session belonged to a common story. June Appal pressed five hundred copies of the recording.

Then, nine years went by and in 1989 *Ancient Creek*

was published as a printed text in an issue of *Hemlocks and Balsams,* a literary journal edited by Allen Speer and published by Lees-McCrae College in Banner Elk, North Carolina. Five hundred copies were printed.

Very few people wound up owning both the recorded and printed versions.

In 1989, a play based on the story was performed by a Whitesburg High School drama group. The June Appal recording and the *Hemlocks and Balsams* text have both been used in college and university courses. The story has been the subject of panel discussions at regional academic conferences as well. I have read the story to groups a few times, in schools and once on the radio.

In Italy in 1994, Annalucia Accardo and Claudio Trovato translated and adapted *Ancient Creek* as a slide-show and video with original music and illustrations by artist Claudio Trovato. The video is part of the ongoing research and music and theatrical performances of the Appalachian Project, a group of faculty and students at the University of Rome. The video was produced by the Centro Internazionale Crocevia in a series titled "Folktales from the South of the World." An accompanying book included essays by Accardo and Cristina Mattiello.

In almost forty years, probably no more than a thousand people have heard or read or seen *Ancient Creek* performed. The story has disappeared from my own thought for years at a time. Then someone might mention it to me. Or I might come across the original vinyl record and hear my own youthful voice speaking the words and the old story will blossom in my mind again.

The story's career in the world is a modest one. But surely modesty is not all bad, and some processes are naturally gradual. We are told that in oral tradition, stories are worded somewhat differently each time they are told. The teller's mood, the particular audience, the atmosphere of the occasion, all influence the narration. Stories, like everything else, evolve. Many writers create books of "original" folk and fairy tales each year and there are large audiences for them. I have always thought that a true folktale comes into being through slow time via the spoken word.

What if a written story evolves, or devolves, in the other direction and somehow returns to an oral tradition? What if such a process might be the writer's intention?

Ancient Creek begins as a written tale but to me it is a pleasing prospect that in time it could evolve into a told tale. If it isn't actually a "folktale" now, maybe, over slow time, it could become one as the text becomes unfixed. Stranger things have happened. Indeed, in folktales, strange things happen all the time. By now, in *Ancient Creek*, King

Condominium the Third is King George Condominium the Third. In the mountainous land of the Ancient Creek rebels, there is Bunker Hill. The King's Men are becoming Red Coats. The Black Duke has become the notorious Duke of Cumberland, oppressor of the Scottish Highlanders after the battle of Culloden in 1746. Appalachian Hall at Holiday Land is now Culloden Hall.

By far, the best part of the story of *Ancient Creek* for me has been the many creative people who have contributed time and talent to produce the series of recordings, publications and performances, and had some fun doing it. Jack Wright edited and mastered the original 1975 recording, ably assisted by storytellers Jeff Kiser, Gary Slemp and Dudley Wilson. The California artist, the late Shera Thompson, rendered in acrylic a colorful mandala with a dogwood blossom at its center that added beauty and meaning to the original *Ancient Creek* album cover, which was designed by Jonathan Greene.

Angie DeBord and Tony Slone and their son Jubal's sustained attention to *Ancient Creek* has been heartening to me over the years. An early review of *Ancient Creek* by environmentalist Tom FitzGerald helped me believe in the story. The large community of friends at Appalshop has made me feel welcome and at home for forty years. Appalshop filmmaker Elizabeth Barret served as Project

Director for the 2012 CD version of the original *Ancient Creek* recording, which has been digitally remastered by Doug Dorschug and is being released concurrently with this book. The cover of both the CD and the book features an original painting by Morgan County artist and friend Pam Oldfield Meade, who created her own colorful vision of Aunt Haze and Ancient Creek.

The essays included here by scholars Kevin Eyster, Annalucia Accardo and the late Jim Wayne Miller have added a significant new dimension to *Ancient Creek*. That these scholars find meaning in the story is both humbling for me and exciting. Their work opens new vistas of thought and offers fresh insights for the author and for readers. Dr. Eyster's discussion of *Ancient Creek* in folkloric terms and Dr. Accardo's political reading compliment each other in unexpected and useful ways. Jim Wayne Miller's "Living into the Land" will be familiar for its eloquence and personal generosity. Thousands of readers remember this beloved poet, essayist, teacher and friend as one of the great writers of his generation. I thank his wife, poet, teacher and my friend Mary Ellen Miller, for permission to reprint Jim Wayne's essay here.

I extend special thanks and appreciation to my sister, Gwynne Norman Griffith, who has been a constant

source of love and support and encouragement in my
efforts to write since we were teenagers.

Nyoka Hawkins and I have created this book together. She is the soul of Old Cove Press, a true artist,
friend and partner who makes beautiful things happen.
Old Cove Press is named for a small cove on her father's
family homeplace in eastern Kentucky.

Contributors

ANNALUCIA ACCARDO teaches American Literature in the Department of European, American and Intercultural Studies at the University of Rome, Sapienza. She is the author of *L'arte di ascoltare: Parole e scrittura in Grace Paley* (*The Art of Listening: Words and Writing of Grace Paley*, 2012) and *Il racconto della schiavitù negli Stati Uniti d'America* (*The Narrative of Slavery in the United States of America*, 1996). Her current research focuses on the role of Buddhism in African American culture.

DEE DAVIS is the founder of the Center for Rural Strategies, a nonprofit organization that seeks to improve economic and social conditions for rural communities through the creative use of media and communications. He has served as president of the Independent Television Service and consultant to numerous private and public agencies. He serves on the board of the Mary Reynolds Babcock Foundation, Fund for Innovative Television, and Feral Arts of Brisbane, Australia. He lives in Whitesburg, Kentucky.

KEVIN I. EYSTER is Professor of English in the Department of Language and Literature at Madonna University in Livonia, Michigan. He has published essays on a number of American writers, including William Faulkner, Eudora Welty, Nella Larsen, August Wilson, and Colson Whitehead. He teaches seminars on American Folklore and Literature and on William Faulkner and Toni Morrison.

JIM WAYNE MILLER (1936–1996) was a poet, fiction writer, essayist, and Professor of German language and literature at Western Kentucky University. A native of North Carolina, he received his Ph.D. from Vanderbilt University in 1965. His books include *Copperhead Cane* (1964), *Dialogue With A Dead Man* (1974), *The Mountains Have Come Closer* (1980), *Vein Of Words* (1984), *Nostalgia for 70* (1986), *Brier: His Book* (1988), and *Newfound* (1989).

GURNEY NORMAN is the author of the folktale *Ancient Creek,* the novel *Divine Right's Trip,* and *Kinfolks,* a collection of short stories. He co-edited the essay collections *Back Talk: Confronting Appalachian Stereotypes* and *An American Vein: Critical Readings in Appalachian Literature.* After graduating from the University of Kentucky in 1959, he studied writing as a Wallace Stegner Fellow at Stanford University with literary critic Malcolm Cowley and the Irish short story writer Frank O'Connor. A former newspaper reporter, he has written and narrated three documentary programs for Kentucky Educational Television that explore Kentucky and Appalachian history, landscape and culture. Three stories from the *Kinfolks* collection have been adapted as short dramatic films, directed by Andrew Garrison. In 2009, Norman was appointed Kentucky Poet Laureate, 2009-2010. He has been a member of the University of Kentucky Department of English since 1979.